HOME SWEET HOME

Colin Smithson

Red Fox

The day the storm began Pa Gumm came in from the fields with a baby lamb.

He put it by the fire to keep warm.

The mother sheep clattered at the door.
She wanted to come in too!

And Ma Gumm let her in.

It was freezing outside. The rest of the flock
rapped at the window.

Pa Gumm let them in.

Pa Gumm worried about his geese, and Ma Gumm worried about her hens. So they brought them in beside the fire as well.

The bullocks called from the barn. So Pa Gumm let them in.

The wind howled but everyone was safe and snug inside.

The storm lasted late into the evening . . .

. . . and past bedtime.

It lasted past breakfast too.

Then it was over.

All the animals went outside.

But in the evening they all came back!

They made themselves at home . . .

. . . and took over the whole house.

Nothing was safe.

Pa Gumm had had enough.

He carried his chair to the barn.
Ma Gumm carried a table.
Then they moved a bed, and bought a new fire.

Now the animals live in the house.

Pa Gumm comes in to feed them.

And Ma Gumm tucks them up in bed.

The Gumms live next door in the barn.
And everyone is happy.

Some bestselling Red Fox picture books

THE BIG ALFIE AND ANNIE ROSE STORYBOOK
by Shirley Hughes
OLD BEAR
by Jane Hissey
OI! GET OFF OUR TRAIN
by John Burningham
DON'T DO THAT!
by Tony Ross
NOT NOW, BERNARD
by David McKee
ALL JOIN IN
by Quentin Blake
THE MOON'S REVENGE
by Joan Aiken and Alan Lee
BAD BORIS GOES TO SCHOOL
by Susie Jenkin-Pearce
WE CAN SAY NO!
by David Pithers and Sarah Greene
MATILDA
by Hilaire Belloc and Posy Simmonds
WILLY AND HUGH
by Anthony Browne
THE WINTER HEDGEHOG
by Ann and Reg Cartwright
A DARK, DARK TALE
by Ruth Brown
HARRY, THE DIRTY DOG
by Gene Zion and Margaret Bloy Graham
DR XARGLE'S BOOK OF EARTHLETS
by Jeanne Willis and Tony Ross
JAKE
by Deborah King